Belinda Blinked 3;

An erotic story of sexual activity, dripping action and even bigger business deals;

Keep following the sexiest sales girl in business as she continues to earn her huge bonus by being the best at removing her tight silken blouse.

Author; Rocky Flintstone;

Contents;

Butch the Sunburnt Kid;

Chapter 1;

London; Thursday 15.55 local time;

Tony nodded and thought,
'Yes she does have great tits,'
but only for a second. What Belinda said made sense and with the massive increase in sales he could easily justify the new sales position to the board.
'OK, let's do this, shall we interview her now?'
Belinda nodded and wondered if Bill in Human Resources would be assisting.
Tony shouted through to Giselle, 'Darling, can you get Bella and Bill in here?'
'Why yes my sweetie pie.' came the response. Belinda looked away in case Tony saw her smirk, 'Wow,' she thought, 'leave the offices for five days and lose the gossip trail.'

Ten minutes later a panting Bella walked through the door.
'Sorry for the delay Tony, but the dam new key cards are all up the creek.'
'Don't worry Bella,' Tony said. 'Would you like a change of job?'
Bella paled; surely Tony wasn't going to sack her for the sake of a few faulty key cards?
Bella shifted restlessly on the white leather couch Belinda had sweated so profusely on at her final job interview. Belinda couldn't say anything; there was a protocol in these things... especially when HR was involved. All she could do was sit back and watch Bella squirm.

'I don't think a few faulty key cards would...'

Tony interrupted, 'Sorry Bella, you misunderstand, we want to offer you a bigger job… reporting directly to Belinda. Key Account Manager, International Sales to be exact, are you interested?'

'You're kidding me… right? squealed Bella, 'Bigger salary, company car, expense account, reporting to Belinda, Amex card… I'd be a fool to say no, so it's yes, yes, yes!'

Belinda laughed, 'Yeah, and lots of work, work, work!'

'I'll take that as a yes,' said Tony. 'Meet me in the leather room in 23 minutes to clear up a few loose ends please.'

'Yes sir!' exclaimed the beaming Bella.

'I'll write Bella a job description this very afternoon and send it to Bill in HR so everything is official.' said Belinda to a purring Tony. How she loved this part of the job.

Bella virtually ran out of the office, bumping into Giselle in the corridor.

'Congrats! Bella welcome to the team!'

'Thanks Giselle, what a week. But hey, what's that on your finger?'

'Oh just a little something Tony gave me.'

'Jeepers,' said Bella, 'it's beautiful, does it come with a date?'

Giselle shrugged at her bosom gal pal.

'I'm very excited, but don't tell Belinda I want her to notice, if you know what I mean!'

'Mum's the word,' said Bella and then looked down at Giselle's stomach, 'sorry, is that the wrong word?'

Giselle punched Bella on the arm, laughed, shook her head and went back into her office.

It was Friday 9.00am when Belinda jumped off the DLR train and into the Millennium Dome building. How she adored it's modernistic curves. Somewhere deep in its winding corridors, Belinda practiced her presentation, mouthing deeply. Suddenly and without any warning a small man dressed completely in black clothing appeared next to her.

'Morning Miss. I need to microphone you up for the show.' the small man dressed in black said in an even tinier voice.

'Funny,' Belinda thought, 'that a man so quiet was in charge of all the sound in the whole of the Millennium Dome building'.

'Oh, of course!' Belinda smiled; after all she'd seen enough episodes of The Generation Game to know what went on behind the scenes. 'I'll guess you'll need to thread the wire under my outer clothing, is that correct?' she said wickedly.

'Yes Miss. That would be super duper.'

'I thought as much.' said Belinda as she ripped off her blouse, revealing her heaving tits which even at that time of the morning were weighing down her brassiere.

The smallish man dressed in black oggled her chest.

'Sorry. Do you need more space to work with, Mr. sound man?'

'No, that's fine.' the small man dressed in black stammered back.

'Come now, if a job's worth doing. I thought you were a professional?'

In a brisk flick, she pinged off her bra and let her magnificent tits fall.

'There. Now you can place the wire anywhere you'd like.'

'Th-th-thank you Miss.' the small man dressed in black muttered as he excitedly lassoed the wire around her neck, then under each tit which he held up by its nipple and finally down her back. Once he was happy with the wires position he used lots of masking tape to affix it in place.

'Now you'll need to attach it somewhere.' Belinda said.

'Y-yes.'

Belinda thrusted forward and shoved her sexy ass into the small man dressed in black's face; after all, he was the perfect size for an eye-full of her hot rear.

The smallish man dressed in black affixed the wireless microphone block onto Belinda's tight white leather skirt, slapped her perfect ass and said; 'All ready to go now, Miss. Break a leg; knock 'em dead! Oh and here's my card... you know, for later!' He winked a smallish wink.

Belinda straightened herself, took the proffered card and moved towards the stage.

'You can call me Alfie by the way.' he shouted. 'Add me on Linkedin and we can connect again.'

Belinda Blinked;

Belinda twisted on her heels, marched onto the stage and in front of her thousands of ladies applauded. Yes, Belinda was dressed to kill, gone was the normal business wear of yesterday. This morning she had a new white linen jacket with a Steele's Pots and Pans lapel badge. On her feet were a pair of Brian Atwood's famous red coloured high heels... a 'haute fashion' statement in itself. Belinda's long glossy black hair had been styled into a high bun; this was a hairstyle many of her audience could associate with. It brought poise and balance to her erotic body. More importantly it still gave her that common, down to earth look but with glamour stamped all over it.

'Good morning ladies!' her voice boomed around the stadium. Belinda wasn't nervous. She always knew she would one day play the O2 and here she was.

'I'm Belinda Blumenthal and I'm the International Sales Director for Steele's Pots and Pans'.

Impressed lady voices rippled through the dome.

'I know you're all wondering - what is new with Steele's Pots and Pans? Well we have just launched a wonderful new range. The Oxy Brillo range and it's a very fine range indeed. Perfect for all your cooking needs; In fact everyone here today will go home with a non-stick tin wok. Look under your seats.'

20,000 ladies scrambled under their uncomfortable plastic chairs and burst into applause, cheering as they grabbed their first prize of the day. Needless to say the presentation was a resounding success.

Outside Belinda caught a taxi back to the offices where she would debrief Tony.

'Boy oh boy,' she thought, 'are things picking up!'

It was a busy Friday morning in London and the traffic was worse than normal, it took ninety minutes to get back to her office. That was bad as she would now be under pressure; her four o-clock appointment with the Duchess at the Ritz Spa was important to her and she could not be late.

Chapter 2;

Epsom Hall;

The Duchess was sitting in the Spa reception when Belinda rushed in a mere five minutes late.
'Terribly sorry My Lady, it's been a very busy morning!'
'Think nothing of it Miss Belinda; I've only just arrived myself.'
Thanks My Lady for doing this today, it's literally my only free afternoon for the next couple of weeks, let's go to the mud room!'
'Miss Belinda, I'm honoured. You're still OK for our shindig at the Isle of Whyte?'
Belinda nodded her head and started stripping off. The Duchess purred with pleasure,
I'm sorry Miss Belinda; just the sight of you undressing sends me into orgasm.' Belinda smiled and she and the Duchess relaxed for the first time that week letting the mud packs do the talking.

'What have you planned for tonight and tomorrow night Miss Belinda? I would like to invite you to a very special dinner party this evening and then to a show jumping championship with a good clubhouse dinner and awards ceremony afterwards. I think you might meet a few of my close circle who would interest you.'
Belinda thought for a moment, she was actually doing nothing this weekend.
'Actually My Lady, I'm free!'
'Splendid, splendid... Miss Belinda!' They both laughed and sat in silence, relaxing in each other's company and sorting out the trivial details a busy weekend always entails.

Two hours later, with her new horse riding clothes, evening gown and a weekend bag of bras and thongs in tow, Belinda and The Duchess motored down to Epsom in her Mercedes. Belinda turned off the main A24 and passed through an impressive gatehouse. The drive was nearly two miles long, and at the end of it was Epsom Hall, a magnificent red brick building dating from Elizabethan times.

'Now Miss Belinda, you will certainly meet my husband Clarence, take no notice of him he's a whimpering fool, rushing after any bit of skirt or thong he can get his hands on. He's been like this since birth, so don't be fooled.'

Belinda nodded, this was exactly the information she needed to know, she didn't want to be seen to be letting herself down in such esteemed company.

'As for the rest of the guests... well you're a bright girl, you can work them out yourself, just one rule... I Miss Belinda am the only one you can fuck tonight.'

Belinda said, 'Yes My Lady.' and retrieved her luggage from the car.

The Duchess opened the heavy wooden door leading to Belinda's chamber. The house was so posh, it didn't have bedrooms. A magnificent four poster bed stood in front of them with drapes which were capable of giving the utmost privacy if needed. The Duchess led Belinda through to the anteroom where the bathroom and clothes closet were located. In its own way it was large with a splendid full sized gilt mirror at one end. She walked over to the W.C. and pushed the handle up instead of down. As if by magic the gilt mirror swung sideways opening into a third room.

The Duchess beckoned Belinda through.

'This, Miss Belinda is my very private boudoir, only my closest associates enter.' The room was decked out in glass mirrors including the ceiling. Elegant mirrored shelving held all the Duchesses sex toys. Belinda counted at least ten different dildos with zinc cases beside them... all ready to go. Exotic lingerie of different colours hung around mixed with shiny rubber clothing, masks and hats. Sexual jewellery was laid out in neat rows waiting for placement in the most private parts of the Duchesses body.

'Miss Belinda, please me by selecting anything you wish and wearing it over the weekend. I especially want you to wear this.' The Duchess pointed at something which looked like a silver bullet. In fact there were two of them. The Duchess pulled down Belinda's skin tight jeans and removed her thong.

'Place these in your vagina and relax, use the lube, it's easier.'
Belinda squirted a decent dollop of lube into her palm.
'No, no, no, Mistress Belinda, far too much... they'll slip out in an instant... it happened to me once in Claridge's tea rooms... a ghastly mess. Poor Clarence was scrabbling all over the place trying to retrieve them.'
Belinda smiled and thought, 'She must have been having one of their famous cream teas, how nice.' The Duchess removed three quarters of the lube and gently massaged it onto Belinda's ass, placed the two bullets in Belinda's palm and said,
'Now roll them so they're lightly covered and pop them in... just like that.'

Belinda complied; it wasn't such a big deal so far and besides it was always good to keep up with the latest technology. Then the Duchess picked up what looked like a small television remote and pressed some buttons. Belinda stood up straight in shock, her vagina was being buzzed by a gently vibrating silver bullet, she breathed in deeply controlling her senses. It was quite fun, no not true, it was great fun she was actually enjoying it.
'Having a good time Miss Belinda?' said the Duchess.
'Come here, My Lady.'
Belinda pulled down The Duchesses trousers and thong, found her clit and started licking her as aggressively as the vibrating bullet in her vagina. The Duchess gasped and increased the bullet's speed; Belinda responded in tempo, she felt like an orchestra being conducted by a mad conductor. However time was not on their side.
'Miss Belinda, please stop, I have guests arriving in fifty minutes, I have to attend to their needs.'
'But My Lady, what about my needs, I need your attention too, please don't desert me?'
The Duchess switched off the remote and the sensation in Belinda's cervix died. They both redressed quickly.
'Follow me, Miss Belinda; I have one last room to show you.'

The Duchess pulled another lever, this time disguised as an ebony penis holding an out of this world necklace with optional nipple clamps, and one of the wall mirrors opened. The Duchess walked through.

'This is my bathroom and closet and through there is my bedroom, so you see my darling Mistress we have interconnecting rooms. Please strip off fully and feel free to explore, I will return in time to dress you for dinner.' With that the Duchess went off to greet the five guests who were arriving imminently. Belinda wandered back to her room and finished stripping off, now was her opportunity to try out some of the more unusual sex items awaiting her pleasure.

Chapter 3;

Dinner at the Duke's table;

Belinda stood to the side of the large drawing room, she and the Duchess had been served drinks by the footman and were waiting for the first guests to make their way down to dinner. Belinda's mouth dropped open, she recognised the man walking through the doorway. It was her Chief Executive, Sir James Godwin. He strolled nonchalantly across the room looking very smooth in his puce dinner jacket. 'Good evening The Duchess, Belinda.' nodding his head at them both.

'Good evening Sir James.' said Belinda attempting to make small talk, 'have you motored down from Windsor this evening?'

'No, no, Clarence and I were doing a bit of clay pigeon shooting down in Dorset, had a devil of a time getting back here... traffic's terrible... always terrible, someone's head in government will roll for it.'

At that precise moment, Belinda's vagina started to tingle, it was one of the bullets. She breathed in deeply and looked at the Duchess. She was smiling playfully at her and mouthed the words, 'Feeling good?' Belinda silently replied,

'Yes My Lady!'

At that moment a tall stately man entered the room.

Belinda Blinked;

Clarence the Duke of Epsom, husband of the Duchess was not as she had imagined.

'Clarence, meet Belinda Blumenthal, she's the one I told you about; Belinda, my husband, The Duke of Epsom.' said the Duchess.

Belinda deeply curtseyed. He looked her up and down hungrily and turned back to his wife.

The Duchess gave Clarence a boring smile and pressed the remote in her pocket. Belinda stiffened to attention immediately; her vagina was once again vibrating as the silver bullet did its dastardly work. She grunted out loud, Belinda couldn't stop the automatic reaction.

'Pardon?' said The Duke.

'Oh, I apologise Lord Duke Clarence, I only meant to say how good looking and stately you are.'

'Yes, well, it is bred into us you know, us aristocrats.'

At that moment Belinda was whisked away by the Duchess to meet the remaining guests. The first, Tara Gold was a television executive and journalist. Then she was introduced to the Duchess's dear male friend Mr. Jim Walters, CEO of Apollo Security Agencies. Lastly she met Mr. Norman Asquith, OBE and City Banker and his companion for this evening the one and only Chiara Montague, fashioner designer to the rich and famous.

At each introduction and with perfect timing, the Duchess pressed the remote sending Belinda into the primary stage of melt down. But she gritted her now flushing pussy; after all there were too many interesting people here for her to make a fool of herself, albeit on the whim of her very close sexual friend the Duchess.

Dinner was perfect, Belinda found herself sitting between Norman Asquith and Jim Walters. They were well matched as they knew of Steele's Pots and Pans and Belinda found the heady mix of security and banking very interesting. She wondered if she was being head hunted by both these men at the same time.

After an exquisite pudding of trifle the guests mingled for fun. Belinda drank some Chardonnay and sought out the company of Chiara Montague and Tara Gold. She chatted loosely to them all the while waiting for something to happen deep inside her.

'So, what do you do Belinda?' asked Chiara.

'I sell Pots and Pans for Sir James.'

'Not that lecher; pardon my French. I'm totally tired of telling him to make contact with my half sister, Penelope. She's the top purchasing executive for the hypermarket chain Fivecarre in France, but he keeps telling me he hates 'frogs', won't have anything to do with them.'

Belinda's eyes then rolled to the top of her head whilst she grabbed her vagina trying to stop the bullet from vibrating free of its moorings.

'Oh no!' shrieked Chiara. 'I think Miss Belinda is ill.'

Belinda tried to steady herself but her vagina was now awash with her own juices, it wouldn't be long before she started pooling on the floor. It got worse, she could now feel both bullets moving all over the place; indeed one of the little buggers had even gotten as far as her G spot. Her watering eyes landed on the silently cackling Duchess who was gleefully stroking all the buttons on the remote like a xylophone.

'Perhaps it was the Chicken Kiev,' mused Sir James. 'if it's not cooked properly it can induce food poisoning through salmonella. Dam those kitchen staff, they've always had it in for us rich people.'

'Well I think we've all had our fill anyway.' said the Duchess.

With that Lord Duke Clarence made a toast to The Queen and everyone gracefully retired for the night.

Back in her chamber Belinda removed her clothing. Her magnificent breasts tumbled out, her nipples free at last started to swell responding to the chemical signals her vagina was sending to her brain.
She needed a good fuck. Remembering the earlier words of the Duchess,
'Only I am allowed to fuck you tonight.'
Belinda decided to wander through the anterooms to her chamber. She only got as far as the sex toy room when she had an idea. Belinda took the long necklace with the nipple clamps and put it on, carefully adjusting the clamps to give a small but decent sensation... there was no need to go too far over the top, especially after what she'd experienced earlier that evening. She then chose two heavy silver chains again with small clamps attached to their ends. One she attached to her vaginal lids and the other she attached to her nipples. Belinda was pleased her nipples were so extended that they could accommodate both the necklace and the glistening silver chain. Finally she chose two long dangling ear rings each ending in a heavy golden penis which pulled her ear lobes to their maximum length. Her outfit complete she collected one of the more attractive strap on dildo's, pulled on the ebony penis handle and jangled her way through to the Duchesses rooms.

She found the Duchess stretched out on her four-poster reading a high society horse magazine.
'My Lady,' whispered Belinda, 'I have come to please you, and for you to please me.' She lay down beside the Duchess and started to fondle her breasts. The Duchess sat up and said,
'No Miss Belinda. I am completely exhausted and we have a very full and riveting day tomorrow, no more action tonight. No more.'
Belinda Blinked;
Crestfallen, Belinda slowly made her way back to her chamber leaving all the chains attached to her body. She would sleep with

them on and enjoy them in her exotic dreams... and dam the Duchess.

Chapter 4;

A topless ride;

Nine-o-clock came and went. Belinda ate her breakfast dressed as instructed in her horse riding clothes and a weary looking Duchess joined her ten minutes later looking ravishing in her full equestrian gear. They set off to Battwood Park where the under-nineteen ladies show jumping trial event was taking place. On arrival The Duchess seemed to know everyone and Belinda was very impressed with her professionalism. Gin and tonics with plenty of ice were served and the first round started. The ten contestants lined up and The Duchess pointed out Penelope Pollet's daughter.

'Takes after her mother I do have to admit,' said the Duchess, 'and speaking of which Penelope should be here by now.' On cue a small disturbance to the left of the stand saw an extremely beautiful and sophisticated lady enter the seating area. The Duchess jumped up and waved her lace handkerchief at her, the beautiful lady smiled and sat directly behind the Duchess and Belinda.
'My Lady, my apologies for my lateness.' said Penelope to the Duchess in a whisper that only Belinda could also hear.
The Duchess replied equally as quietly, 'My Mistress Penelope, do not worry, you are just in time.'

Belinda Blinked.

'Mistress Penelope, please let me introduce my Mistress Belinda, the one I've told you about.' said the Duchess.

Penelope took Belinda's hand and whispered, 'Welcome to our exclusive club my Mistress Belinda, enchanté!'

'Merci my Mistress Penelope.' replied a slightly shaken Belinda catching on extremely quickly. The Duchess turned to Belinda, winked at her and said,

'Now let's enjoy the jumping!'

Katerina Pollet jumped her heart out and came a very worthy eighth.

'A very good result for her Penelope,' said the Duchess, 'now let's have a glass of cold Australian Chardonnay in celebration!'

Penelope Pollet laughed and replied, 'You English are always the same with your ice cold Australian Chardonnay! ' Belinda laughed and moved the subject onto Steele's Pots and Pans.

'Certainment Belinda, I have no problem in giving your company a trial. If you can organise to see me in my offices in Paris we can get started.'

Belinda nodded her head enthusiastically.

'I think also you will need to make it an overnight stop, n'est ce pas?'

By six thirty that afternoon having seen Miss Penelope Pollet's daughter, Katrina win the Best Effort prize and a respectable dinner, Belinda and the Duchess were motoring back up to Epsom. It was another glorious early evening so the sun roof was down letting the warm breeze blow their natural hair behind them.

'This is idyllic Miss Belinda,' said the Duchess as she slipped her hand onto Belinda's covered breasts. She slowly opened Belinda's shirt and unclasped her bra. Belinda's breasts did what they did best and tumbled forwards into the Duchess's grip. Bony fingers clutched the bare flesh and gently massaged it. Belinda concentrated on her driving whilst enjoying the attention. After twenty minutes the Duchess pulled down Belinda's jodhpurs and started to work on her g-spot. There was no hurry, and fortunately for the now half naked Belinda there was absolutely no lorry traffic and very few cars.

Belinda did have to stop for fuel, but as it was an attended service station, she felt she didn't have to button up. She thought she'd give the lad serving a decent tip, a good view of her tits, vagina and clit which the Duchess helpfully exposed when directed. They both hoped this would make his Sunday lunchtime in the local pub with his unruly and randy contemporaries. She and the Duchess enjoyed his reaction to Belinda's bare body and giggled filthily when he overfilled the car by not paying attention to his task.

Belinda turned into the Duchesses long driveway and steered the Mercedes into a small glade and parked. She smiled at the Duchess and thanked her for a brilliant weekend whilst removing the Duchesses red coat, cravat, cream shirt, and brassiere. Naked except for her boots and jodphurs the Duchess lay back on the passenger seat and let Belinda gently lick her clitoris. Belinda then pulled her riding crop out of the glove box and flicked its scarlet end onto the Duchesses vagina. She moaned in ecstasy calling out for more, Belinda obliged her, but never altering the tempo or force of the riding crop, it was a stimulant and nothing more.

After twenty minutes of this punishment the Duchess was a quivering wreck. Her legs were now spread as far apart as she could make them and her massive nipples were shivering with anticipation. She could wait no longer,
'Please, please, please Mistress Belinda bondage my breasts and nipples as you have my vagina and clitoris'. Belinda gladly obliged her, tapping her tits one after the other like a tight snare drum in the Lord Mayor's Show, but each time getting closer to the aureole and eventually the nipples themselves.
'I say Mistress Belinda, I'd like to spread my rather longish legs onto the dashboard...' screamed the Duchess

'Why yes, of course, how silly of me, I've always thought this Mercedes model had very short foot wells.' replied Belinda hospitably.

A deep resonant groan emanated from the prostrate Duchess, she gushed copiously as her orgasm climaxed and Belinda wiped the golden liquid off her right eyelid. The Duchesses steel tipped boot heels moved up and down the walnut veneered dashboard leaving two, scratches etched deeply into the polished surface. The car hire company would have a fit Belinda thought.

The Duchess was now orgasming each and every minute, the car seat was becoming wet with female juices and the sounds of her slipping and sloshing ass was starting to drown out her orgasmic moans. It couldn't have gone on forever and Belinda eventually pulled her own clothes back on and threw the red riding jacket over the now delirious Duchess. She kept repeating to Belinda how she never had a car ride just like it, and now fully understood why you rode in cars. Belinda carefully drove the last couple of hundred yards up to the mansion as the Duchess was in no fit state to wear her seatbelt. She parked round the back and left the still naked Duchess writhing on the gravel with her clothes strewn around her. After all she had staff and servants for this sort of thing and Belinda had to get back to central London. The Duchess regally waved her wrist despite the sexually devastated state Belinda had left her in. Belinda cheerily said her goodbyes and was gone in a whisk of a lamb's tail.

Belinda was driving fast, well over the speed limit, but after all she was in the Duchess's territory and now knew Lord Duke Clarence personally so she was above the law. She negotiated the steep corners and curves like the Bond girl she truly was.

Suddenly, she skidded off the road, smashing into an ancient oak tree coming to a stop in a deep ditch. The noise was horrific and there wasn't a soul for at least 25 miles. She lay there motionless and unblinking in the smoking car...

Chapter 5;

Accident or Emergency?;

Belinda's watering eyes slowly opened as she suffocated on the merciful air bag. She sat up in the car wreckage.
Belinda Blinked.
'For fuck sakes,' her mind told her angrily, 'a flat tyre, well there's only one thing for it.'
Belinda removed her disheveled blouse and threw herself onto the ground. Flinging her hair back, she did her best 'damsel in distress' act, making sure her tits were protruding out of her somewhat skimpy bra. She was on her knees for a good long while waiting for a passing car, but at least her exposed breasts were being kept snug by the sun blushed tarmac.
Two hours later a 1960s mustang stopped next to her helpless body and out jumped Marko Ourigues. Marko Ourigues was Brazilian, and he knew it. Impossibly handsome, he was the living example that God was a Brazilian. Full of poise, impeccable manners and, he thought, to die for in bed. He also didn't settle for the average, his taste in women was that of high class, and the lady he had just seen lying in the middle of the road was high class. Everything about her was sexual, from the quality of her clothing to the gloss of her hair and the way she wore those riding boots. He knew he had to have her, and he knew she wouldn't deny him.

'You must save me, kind sir. I have a flat tyre.'
'Not from what I can see.' he said in perfect English, albeit with a slight Boston accent, as he stared at her now heaving breasts.
Nevertheless Marko Ourigues agreed to drive Belinda back to his central London apartment to check she had no internal organ damage. And as they thundered through the world famous scenic countryside the pair got to chatting freely.
'You may not know of me in person,' said the Brazilian/Boston voice, 'but how's Bella?'

Belinda Blinked.

'But how do you know Bella? Come to think of it, how do you know me?' spluttered the for once flummoxed Belinda Blumenthal.
'You're reputation proceeds you Ms. Blumenthal. The second I saw your tits in the wing mirror I knew it was the queen of pots and pans.' he replied bowing his head and smiling his deep Brazilian smile. 'You were helpless and I was your Brazilian prince charming here to save the day.'
Belinda smiled and thought, 'If he gets any more patronising, I'll smack him one, potential customer or not!'
'Belinda, I can see I've offended you, I apologise, not everyone I meet is as sharp witted as yourself.' said an intensely uncomfortable and now slightly worried Marko.
Belinda smiled and thought, 'He is handsome. And if he's a lover of Bella he can't be that bad in bed.'
'Continue.' she mouthed whilst her tongue wet her lips.

'My business takes me all over the world and this week I'm in London, Athens and Moscow. I'm a world famous plastic surgeon and I had the pleasure of Miss Bella's company in the good ole US of A not too long ago. I was there as a high ranked guest of a guy called Stirling.'
'Jim Stirling?' squealed an excited Belinda.
'You know of the little chap too?'
'Know of him? He's been inside me on more than one continent! At least I think he has.' Belinda murmured to the buzzing fly around her head.
It all made sense; Belinda owed Marko big time for saving her from Stirling's maggot cock in Texas USA all those days ago. Suddenly a comfortable silence settled between the two of them.

Back at Marko's London mansion block on Harley Street, Belinda lay back on his wolf fur rug in front of a fake but very realistic looking fire place. He had given her a caipirinha cocktail and secretly hoped his semen tasted as bitter sweet.

Belinda removed her red jacket, she didn't want wine stains or anything else for that matter spoiling it, and it was far too new to be sent to the dry cleaners. With Belinda now half naked, Marko concentrated on her jodhpurs. They didn't put up much of a fight as they'd already been off earlier in the day and were getting to know the score... so to speak.

He slowly and extremely gently traced a path with his finger up to the base of Belinda's vagina. There his finger stopped, just like a car at a railway crossing, waiting for the barrier to be lifted. After a minute his finger continued on its journey;

'The barrier has obviously been raised,' Belinda thought astutely as a very grateful Marko took the opportunity to pleasure Belinda's clitoris with his tongue. She relaxed and let Marko's tongue do the talking.

Suddenly and without any warning the Brazilian flipped Belinda onto her stomach and started tapping her back with a reflex hammer.

'Does this hurt Belinda?'

'Not yet.' she said wickedly. Marko nodded, looking serious.

'Oh it was such an aphrodisiac watching a man take his job seriously,' Belinda's mind said, 'take good note you shoddy RSMs.' Marko's final test was to ensure her heart had not been damaged in the car crash. He placed the stone cold stethoscope on her left breast. All he could hear was the thundering of Belinda's desire. Content, Marko returned to ravaging her clit whilst she chewed on the soft, short dark hair on his head. Belinda soon started in search of similar material lower down his athletic body. She read his body hair like brail; around his nipples and all the way down his snail trail to his belt.

She cracked it off and pulled his trousers and speedo trunks away from his torso. His manhood sprang up before her and she had to admit Brazilians were well endowed. Perhaps he had modelled Jim Jr. part II on himself; anything was possible in the plastics game.

Belinda pointed at her boots and said, 'Help me take these off.'

Marko bent over, took the first boot between his legs and pulled. Belinda pushed her foot higher and squashed his balls. He groaned with pleasure, Belinda pushed harder, Marko pulled harder, and plop, the riding boot was off. They repeated exactly the same procedure for the second boot. With her toes finally free Belinda very neighbourly invited his penis into her vagina. She let him fuck her with vigour as Belinda picked up a fancy brass fireplace poker, struck him on the ass and started to scream in delight as he responded. This continued for at least the next five minutes, the Brazilian's cock was now so big she couldn't help shouting out her desire.

A loud knocking noise from the ceiling with the words, 'SHUT IT' brought her back to reality; she choked back the next scream and bore her pounding in silence. Eventually Sr. Ourigues came and collapsed into her open arms.

Belinda grabbed Marko's still erect cock and took it into her mouth. She wanted to thank him for her first orgasm, so unselfishly given but she was always taught not to speak with her mouth full. He groaned and stood his ground whilst Belinda attacked him with her lips, teeth and tonsils.

'God you're refreshingly good, Belinda,' he exhaled, 'so, so, good! I want you to join me soon in Rio, please consider it!'

For the second time that afternoon,

Belinda Blinked;

Chapter 6;

Mr. Claus Bloch;

'Mr. Bloch will see you now Miss Blumenthal.' Belinda followed the manservant through the doors into a large morning room of the Grosvenor hotel.

Belinda was feeling deliciously excited about this meeting with her new contact. The new contact was none other than the direct retail door to door and coffee morning organisation's CEO and Managing Director, Claus Bloch. The child of young Austrian sweet hearts who had found themselves displaced by the war in Europe, Bloch looked around forty-nine, was single and successful in many different direct sales fields.

Amongst his personal friends he was known as a bit of a Casanova, but this was not general knowledge. They had met briefly at the O2 where he kissed Belinda's hand at length and thanked her for her excellent presentation.

'Ahh Belinda.' exclaimed Mr Bloch, 'thank you for coming.' Belinda curtsied as it seemed the only thing to do.

'Please sit down... here.' He waved his open hand to a very low slung but pretty armchair where no doubt he would be able to observe her body in its entirety. Belinda obliged him, opening her legs just a fraction and placing her briefcase on her lap.

'Hit me,' Bloch said, 'In the nicest possible way of course.' he smiled and Belinda opened her briefcase and took out her proposal paperwork.

'That about wraps a very successful morning's business my dear Belinda.' Bloch smiled for the umpteenth time and clapped his hands. The manservant appeared and Bloch ordered luncheon on the terrace. Claus and Belinda wandered over to the trellis covered outside area and sat down.

'No doubt you know of my background,' said Claus, 'but I know so little of yours dearest Belinda.' Belinda smiled and replied, 'There's not much to hear about, born in Kent, small country primary school, larger local schools as I grew up and finally University in Central London and work... mostly sales at Typhoid Crockery Holdings in Canterbury, and here I am today.

'Fascinating Belinda, how wonderful to have been given the gift of such a simple upbringing, it gives you the ability to connect with ordinary people doing ordinary things. People like my wonderful ladies.'

Belinda nodded in agreement and thought, 'Harness the ordinary person and you could rule the world. Just look at Bella.'

A simple lunch of destressed lettuce leaves and blue cheese fish mousse was served accompanied by a single bottle of champagne. It really was something; well, let's say spectacular, after all Belinda travelled the world and knew her onions when it came to exotic food.

'A toast to our continued success Belinda.' proclaimed Claus Bloch with his glass held high. They touched glasses, Claus clumsily spilt some champagne over Belinda's cocktail dress and it quickly soaked through her brassiere to her breasts. As if they were waiting for that exact signal Belinda's nipples started to expand.

'My dear, I'm so sorry, let me dry you off.' Claus took his napkin and started to gently dab Belinda's breasts. He could feel her nipples rising and said,

'It's no good, the dress needs to be hung up and dried properly.' He pulled down Belinda's straps and skillfully maneuvered it to the ground. He then hung the cocktail dress over a spare ornately woven wooden chair where it would dry of its own accord in the warmish breeze.

'That's much better... my goodness, what fine breasts you have, may I touch them?'

Belinda nodded, and wondered how far Claus would go. He had obviously agreed to her business terms and if Belinda played this little adventure correctly she would sew up the deal very tightly indeed. Seconds later her brassiere fell to the floor and Belinda's breasts were once again in action. He bent his body to delicately tease the saluting nipples with his lips.

Meanwhile his hands weren't idle and in one fluid motion Claus whisked her dental floss vaginal garment down her legs and over her red high heels. He began to explore her already slightly wet vagina with his fingers and soon located her clitoris and then her G spot.

Using an ancient Chinese technique few people in the Western world knew about he started to massage both sensual areas at the same time. It was indeed the very same technique which had gained his reputation as a Casanova, few women, if any, had ever complained about his attentions.

Belinda couldn't help it, she opened her legs wider and wider, the sensation was exquisite, like drinking the nectar of the Gods. Claus piled on the pressure, Belinda started to beg for an orgasm, but this was the secret of the ancient Chinese technique, no orgasm could climax whilst this method of stimulation was being applied. Belinda raised her hands to her head and removed the clips holding up her bun hairstyle. Her long black glossy hair cascaded over her body bringing her mentally back to a pre Neolithic state.

She started to snarl instead of groan, she was becoming part animal and part human, but very much needing to orgasm. Now totally naked apart from her red heels, Belinda pushed Bloch away from her, he removed his hand from her vagina, she snarled again and started to rip his clothing off his body. He bowed in deference and quickly assisted her basic actions.

Once Belinda had Bloch naked she went on all fours and snarled, 'Fuck me doggy style!'

Bloch jumped onto her and stuffed his erect penis into her vagina. She roared in theriomorphic passion, gnashing her teeth and scratching the gravel like the wild beast she had become. He grabbed her bouncing tits and held on tight. Belinda climaxed almost immediately emitting a long heart rending snarl which ended in a whimper. In a flash the cave woman had gone and a highly sex charged, extremely sophisticated modern young business woman was left in her place.

Belinda slowly regained her mind and concentrated on tightening her cervix, she was going to give Claus Bloch the sexual experience of his life.

Chapter 7;

The Chocolate fountain;

Tuesday morning started sunny and bright. Today was Brussels, Alfonse Stirbacker in actual fact. He was her first client and conquest on that fateful Sunday afternoon in the maze at Sir James Godwin's country home.

'Wow,' she thought, 'how the business had moved on from then.' Sitting at her desk Belinda quickly looked at her appointments for the rest of the week. She planned to get back to London on Wednesday night giving her all day Thursday to visit one of her Managers out in the field and Friday morning was for paperwork. Friday afternoon was however Glee Team time where they all caught up on the week's antics.

She rang Jim Thompson her sales admin guy and asked him to set up a visit with Ken Dewsbury for the Thursday.

'Righty ho,' said Jim, "I'll presume you'll fly into Leeds Bradford early morning and back to Heathrow late that night?'

'Sounds like a tough days work Jim, but yes, that'll do the trick nicely. Oh, tell Ken to pick me up from the airport around 9.30ish and then back again to get that late 8.00pm flight.'

'Wilco, Belinda.'

'Thanks Jim you're a star!'

Belinda checked her bag onto the Brussels shuttle and walked to the departure area. She was feeling relaxed and with a bit of luck they'd have their first bottle of wine ordered by 1.30. The flight was uneventful and Alfonse was in the arrivals hall waiting for her. They kissed, like old established lovers and Alfonse took her bag and hand.

It was actually 1.33 on the dot as the waiter set down the first bottle of green crisp white wine on the table. They'd ordered moule frites and a delicious chocolate dessert which Belinda became particularly enthralled with.

'Alfonse, this is soo good, do you do business with the manufacturers…. I presume they are Belge, after all you do make the best chocolate in the world!'

'Kind words Belinda, and yes, funnily enough their Managing Director is a very good friend of mine. I'll give her a call and see if she can get the two of us a private tour around the factory this afternoon. But now we must get back to my offices to tie up the paperwork.'

Alfonse efficiently shuffled the last of his papers, shut his briefcase, looked at Belinda across the large green leather desk and confirmed the deal.

'It's done, 7000 units ordered, complete with your input of 20% marketing assistance. We'll stop off at your hotel to allow you to freshen up and then onto the chocolate factory! Madeliene Chocolat is waiting for us with much anticipation I must add.'

Belinda nodded attentively, '7,000 units in one hit was fantastic, she would page Tony and Jim the minute she got back to the hotel.' she thought smiling.

Forty minutes later saw Alfonse's red Ferrari parked outside the front gates of Madeleine Chocolate. Belinda was surprised, it didn't look like a big place, she'd expected gleaming stainless steel vats of hot runny chocolate which would flow into Easter egg moulds or chocolate bar cartons, ready for sale throughout the wider world. Alfonse looked at her bemused face, grinned and said,

'It's a very bespoke operation, her biggest sale is chocolate fountains… Madeleine is the world's leader in viscous chocolate.'

Belinda's heart sank, she'd been hoping for a few freebie chocolate bars to bring back to the offices, the Glee Team were big chocolate aficionados' and were always looking for the next aphrodisiac.

A powerful, masculine looking, blonde woman strode across the parking area and greeted Alfonse like an old, but forever discarded, lover.

'Madeleine darling, please meet Belinda Blumenthal, my pots and pans supplier.'

Belinda blushed; it was a horrible introduction to someone whom she was somewhat attracted to physically, her job really didn't do her many favours in the status league. Now if she'd worked for a perfumerie company from the south of France...

'Belinda... adorable, you are very chic looking... with your figure, I bet you don't even sniff ze chocolat!'

Belinda laughed, feeling instantly settled by this charming woman. 'Madame Madeleine, thank you so much for organising this very impromptu tour of your facilities.'

Madeleine Chocolat looked at Belinda carefully and thought, 'Zis one iz too good to share with Alfonse, I think we'll skip ze production and go poolside.' Her mind made up Madeleine strode off arm in arm with Belinda leaving Alfonse scurrying along behind.

Up in the deserted control room Madeleine showed Belinda her chocolate empire, she pointed out the various hydraulic siphons which contoured the chocolate into the living fluid which had made her company's name throughout the world. She calmly pointed out the tortuous route the flowing chocolate took until it decanted effortlessly into a large swimming pool structure.

'Now my Belinda,' Madeleine said, 'ave you ever experienced flowing chocolate on your bare skin?'

Belinda Blinked;

They'd both undressed in an ante room far below the control room where Alfonse sat waiting to see the show. He was truly a voyeur and he liked nothing better than seeing stunningly beautiful and naked women make love to each other. The fact they were doing it under a chocolate fountain was an unbelievable bonus. He secretly hoped the security cameras footage would appear on U Tube in the not too distant future. He'd certainly subscribe.

Madeleine gently led the naked Belinda up the slope and into the pool. Glouping chocolate covered her toes, her calves and suddenly her vagina. Belinda put her hands into the running liquid and tasted the voluptuously velvet concoction. It was chocolate, but not as she knew it.

'Do you like Belinda? This is our Quantro flavoured variety... one of my favourites, absolutely delightful for licking off the skin of a lover. It does very well in Texas and Californicatia... you know, the USA...'

Belinda swooned; the intoxicating alcohol had done its intended work. Madeleine calmly caught her before she was immersed completely in the swirling liquid. She laid her on the side of the chocolate fountain pool and started to gracefully lick her body. With her legs splayed wide Madeleine was able to lick Belinda's clitoris clean before starting on her somewhat large vaginal lids. Belinda's tits awoke her with the urgent chemical signals they'd earlier sent to her mind's eye. She sat up slowly and touched Madeleines extended breasts, the nipples responded, covered as they were in luscious chocolate Belinda had no option but to lick them clean. It was an act of deference, abeyance to the ancient Gods of nipples and chocolate. Belinda felt she'd died and gone to heaven, she became entranced and slowly worked her way down the naked body in front of her, slurping as she went; there would be no need for any sort of dinner that evening.

It was a perfect dance of two newly introduced females discovering each other and Alfonse was thoroughly enjoying it. Madeleine was taking the lead, her masculinity had demanded it of her and Belinda was willing to defer. Stretched out as she was on the edge of the chocolate poolside, Belinda was enjoying the penetrating fingers of her host. Her clit was now oh so wet; she orgasmed, once, twice, thrice. In return she bit Madeleine's protruding nipples extremely hard, sounds of ecstasy emanated from the woman's lips each time she clamped harder. The chocolate had done its worst, now it was hard personal sex that drove the two women onward and upward to sexual fulfilment.

Chapter 8;

A fucking good time;

'This is my private club.' said Alfonse sloppily licking his fingers as the taxi drew up outside a very imposing stone building somewhere in the centre of Brussels. The taxi ride had been short.
Alfonse led Belinda, dressed in her long black evening gown with an extremely low cleavage and backless cut which just showed the top of her black string thong, up the wide stone steps. They were immediately shown to the library. Belinda looked around sensing that this was no ordinary reading room with its chairs and reading tables. She studied the other 18 guests, they were all couples, the men were older and the women were younger, they looked extremely ravishing, perhaps they were all business associates just like her.

'Do you do remember my last few words to you in the maze when I invited you to Brussels?' asked Alfonse.
'Yes Alfonse, I do, you said, "All our ladies are expected to be properly dressed... at least when they arrive." Am I correct?'
'Absolutely, and now you will understand the full meaning of my words!'
Belinda was intrigued, is this when they retired to a private members room and he had his wicked way with her? How pathetically boring; especially after this afternoon's excitement.
At that moment a Butler advanced to the centre of the room. 'Mes Dames, si vous plait!'
Alfonse whispered to Belinda, 'The game begins, please stand on the chair, I will guide you, as you may not understand the rules.'

Belinda did as she was told and looked around; the nine other ladies were doing exactly the same.

The Butler shouted, 'Messieurs!'
Immediately all the men removed their clothes, even their socks, throwing them onto the floor.
The Butler shouted 'Avancez!'
A naked Alfonse whispered, 'Remove your dress Belinda.'
Belinda complied and thought, 'this is more like it Alfonse... how quaint, me and nine others.'

The ten now completely naked ladies stood on their chairs wearing only their high heels with their clothing also scattered on the floor around them. The Butler shouted, 'Avancez' once more and red suited valets appeared in unison and cleared the floor of all the discarded garments. Unbeknown to the contestants the club would immediately send them to a charity organisation for distribution to its shops throughout Belgium.
Seconds later the Butler shouted, 'Decendez Une!'
At that command all the ladies stepped down from their chairs. The Butler then shouted,
'Decendez Deux!
Alfonse together with the other nine men helped the ladies onto their backs ensuring they were spread-eagled across the library reading tables.
'Allez!' was the final command the Butler needed to utter as the room descended into a fucking frenzy. Belinda very soon had her dangling legs wide apart and Alfonse was fucking her like a mad thing.
'I've only got about three minutes with you,' Alfonse barked out a deep cough making Belinda think he was going to exit this life and continued, 'and then I've got to move onto the lady on your right. All these men are well versed operators in their own business fields,'

Belinda made sure her cervix was clamped tightly around his long cock for she needed to give Alfonse a good time as he was the reason she was here. Her flexing vagina worked his penis hard. She felt excited, the opportunity to meet nine other contacts as seriously connected as Alfonse didn't arise every day and she was going to make the most of it.

After about four minutes the Butler shouted, 'Allez encore!' The grunting and moaning, with the occasional screams from a couple of very excited ladies, stopped as the men withdrew and moved onto the next table. As her new partner penetrated her, he passed her his business card.

'Oh!' she thought, 'The Minister of Trade for Belgian Colonies, how useful.' She took his card in her teeth and once again set about tightening herself to give Monsieur Rideaux the ride of his week.

'Merci Madame.' He panted as his four minutes expired without ejaculation.

'Think nothing of it Monsieur.' Belinda huskily replied, trying to dampen her desire for an orgasm and feeling exceedingly glad he'd been able to control himself properly.

The words, 'Allez encore!' echoed around the library again. The men moved on and Belinda thought,

'I've heard of speed dating, but this is ridiculous. Giselle and Bella would love it, perhaps we should try speed fucking in London?'

Around the room Belinda could see that most of the women were not up to her level of concentrated sex. One lady indeed was now just giving blow jobs. How defeatist... it wouldn't take much for her to be soaked in semen Belinda thought wickedly.

Her thoughts were discarded as her third partner of the evening penetrated her vagina. He was a lithe looking, olive skinned, youngish man with a medium length haircut to be envied. As he entered her she inspected his business card closely. It said, Aldo Fellini, Direttore Commerciale, Inca Supermercatos SpA.

'Bingo!' she thought and tightened her lids hard, it only took Sr. Fellini two minutes to come and with his release Belinda let herself have the pleasure of her first orgasm that evening. They clasped each other tightly, enjoying the combined sensations of sexual release. However the four minutes were over too soon and Belinda reluctantly let Aldo Fellini continue his journey around the room. Instinctively she knew they'd meet again, she'd make sure of it!

Twenty five minutes later the Butler held his hands above his head and shouted
'Finis!'
After a few minutes all the library members were back sitting on their chairs as if nothing had happened. The only clue to the sexual mayhem of the previous hour was the nakedness of the participants.
The men stood up and the ladies joined them. They then casually left the room chatting to each other about the unfortunate performance of the Euro. Outside, ten black Range Rover Evoques were waiting to whisk the couples back to their hotels. A crowd of press photographers had gathered at this point to record the naked library members leaving the building. It was a biannual event and the Belgian tabloids never missed the sexy photo opportunity it gave them.
Alfonse wiggled his rampant cock at them and whispered in Belinda's ear, 'Behave as if you were fully dressed, give them a polite wave, and smile!' Belinda grinned and hoped her M.D. Tony didn't get the Belgian newspapers too often.

As Belinda's luck would have it, their car was the last in the queue. That meant maximum exposure to the press corp. showing her completely naked body. They crowded round taking full frontal, ass and breast shots similar to their actions at the Oscars.
'Madame, votre nom si vous plait?' they shouted. Belinda didn't answer as she wanted to remain Madam X, to keep the game going. Little information made them even hungrier.
The doors to the Range Rover opened and Alfonse and Belinda escaped the press pack.
'Front page on tomorrow's tabloids, I bet,' said Alfonse. 'My newly divorced wife will have a field day.' He laughed and kissed Belinda's juicy nipples one after the other for the duration of the journey to her hotel, however he really did miss the chocolate.

Chapter 9;

Yorkshire;

Alfonse had left around 2.00ish in the morning saying he had an
early flight to Ireland where they were intending to source an
independent manufacturer of high quality butter. As a result
Belinda was left to board the flight alone. How she longed for Hazel
and a tumble in B2...
Ken Dewsbury waited dutifully in Leeds Bradford airport arrivals for
his boss. Ken saw her before she saw him and he thought once
again what a magnificent creature she was.
'Hi Ken!' shouted Belinda. 'Tell me more about this little problem
with our biggest UK customer.'
Ken nodded sheepishly, he was grateful for the Bosses help, he was
in deep water and he didn't know what to do, never mind where to
go. He wasn't built for confrontation with the famously combative
distribution supervisor and Trade Union boss, Andy Milston of
Shakespeare Retail Stores.

They entered the massive distribution centre unsure of where to
find Milston's office as Ken had only previously called on him in
Worksop where the companies head office was based. A canteen
was opposite them and Belinda went in to ask where Mr Milston's
whereabouts was. The thinish tea lady called Ethel pointed up some
fire escape-like stairs and said,

'Good luck lass... you'll need it!'
Belinda said, 'Thanks!' wondering what she meant about the luck
part of her answer. But her information was good and Belinda soon
found Milston's office.. Ken knocked on the door and they entered.
'Mr Milston sir, I have the pleasure of introducing my Boss, Belinda
Blumenthal; Boss, Mr Andy Milston.'
A big, red, round faced man got up from the desk he was sitting
behind and came forward with outstretched hand. He was about

60ish, bald with a largish beer belly and well-trimmed finger nails. He thought himself a bit of a dandy when it came to women.

'Pleased to meet thee, Belindaaa. Sit thee down please. Ken, big titties Matilda at head office wants to talk to you on the phone about some wrong invoices.'

Ken shook his head, 'More bloody wrong invoices, I swear to God I spend more time with that woman than I do with my wife.'

Belinda Blinked;

That was the first reference Ken Dewsbury had ever made to being married, whatever next she thought.

As Ken left the room to take the call Belinda noticed the whole office wall was a sheet of glass looking into the busy canteen full of lorry drivers in dirty blue overalls.

'This must be how he controls his workforce.' she thought, as a wicked idea flashed across her brain.

'Now then Ms. Blumenthallll, Steele's Pots and Pans have a problem wit' treatin' us lorry driver folk with respect and not ignoring us.' barked Mr Milston.

Belinda blinked once more. What had Ken let happen? She always respected distribution people, they could make or break a supplier's sales to any company if they felt they weren't being treated fairly.

Belinda had made the decision back on the plane to travel thong less throughout Yorkshire and she secretly thanked the Norse gods that she had. Belinda moved her legs apart and quietly hitched her skirt upwards, making sure Andy could see directly in it. It was his office and he was the union, so he slightly moved his chair to get a better view. Andy could now see the top of her pale thighs, but couldn't see any signs of underwear. He continued,

'Now then, do you realise this is the first time your Mr Dewsbury has set foot in this depot....' Andy looked up her legs again, 'Good God,' he thought to himself, 'she's come to my meeting bareback. Well I never!' Andy immediately forgot his increasing rant and wasn't at all put out about Belinda's state of undress; but he'd been flummoxed and didn't know how to capitalise further on it. Andy racked his brains and came up with a quick strategy.

'Can't have theet blouse chaffing those delicate nipples, now, can we.' he said. Belinda dutifully opened her blouse and unclasped her skimpy string bra.

'Good God, what magnificently well-formed titties you have Belindaaa.'

He took them firmly in both his hands and felt their dead weight. He moved them to the right and then left, watching how they always bounced back to their original position. He sadly thought about his Missus. She hardly ever took hers out very often these days.

Years of self-control melted with his continued handling of Belinda's tits and Andy Milston, Trade Union boss of the TGWU union broke his own rules. He touched Belinda's now completely exposed clitoris and started to massage it, crudely, as he was, by his own admission, no expert.

'That's right,' Belinda thought, 'fall under my business woman's spell.'

Andy massaged the little nub of oily skin and enjoyed Belinda getting wetter and wetter, licking his fingers the odd time or two. Belinda realized she was going to get no release from him, but she needed him satisfied, no matter how much she yearned for his cock up her. Andy started to concentrate big time on her tits, sucking them, rolling his fingers up and down her extending nipples, pulling them and eating them as best he could. He was like a horny pig in muck.

'My God Belindaaa, you're so receptive!'

That was his last words for a good half an hour as he manfully brought Belinda to a false climax every few minutes now using his fingers, tongue, lips and nose. Never once did he remove any of his clothes and more importantly never once did he remove his cock from his stained and straining dirty blue overalls.

Belinda smiled as she watched all the lorry drivers gawp at her from the canteen, unbeknown to the very busy Andy Milston TGWU chief. She could give the Home Secretary some tips she mused. But as a man of self-control, eventually Milston's true nature kicked in. He sucked Belinda's tits for another two minutes and then slowly, but sadly, helped her to dress.

'Belindaaa, firstly, thank you. And secondly, can I have a small memento to remind me of your visit?'

'Why certainly Andy, I think I've got a couple of company pens in my briefcase.' replied a curious Belinda.

'Please don't think me silly, or come to that, soft, but I'd like that there string bra.'

'Belinda laughed, 'That's not silly Andy, it's a compliment... take it now.'

Belinda threw the bit of black material to Andy who deftly caught it, smelt her sweat on it and quickly stuffed it into his overalls pocket almost afraid Belinda might change her mind and give him the pens.

'Thanks Belindaaa.' said Andy, 'I owe thee dinner sometime, or whatever...' he finished lamely.

'Andy, don't be concerned, you do a great job for us... you know that, just keep up the good work.'

Andy smiled, 'Nice of you to appreciate us at last, Belindaaa.'

Leaving the office Belinda caught the eye of a gob smacked Ken Dewsbury. As she passed him and all the workforce she said;

'I don't think you'll be having any problems Ken with this lot from now on.' as Belinda jumped into his car.

There was still three hours left before Belinda's flight and Ken suggested she have a refreshing shower before her departure. Belinda agreed and Ken drove back to the outskirts of Leeds. It was in a student district, near Headingly cricket ground, where he turned the diesel Audi down a narrow back street and parked up outside a row of old terraced houses.

'I own these,' he said proudly, 'been in the family for over a hundred years now.'

Belinda Blinked;

Chapter 10;

Ken Dewsbury's Cellar;

The cellar door scraped open noisily as Ken ushered Belinda into his spare basement flat.

'Sorry it's not the Ritz Boss, but it's got a shower and drinks, so you should be fine.' Ken said. Belinda looked around; there was a widescreen, fairly newish TV, two sofas, a table and matching chairs and a well used dartboard. The low ceiling made it look more cramped than it was. A male domain she guessed, perhaps Ken's knocking shop on a good day? Mind you it didn't say much for the standard of bird he attracted if this was where it all happened.

Ken led Belinda through to the bathroom area. In the corner was a well-used toilet, a grotty dirty plastic shower cubicle and a sink. A strong smell of permanent rising damp was probably the clue as to why it wasn't rented out.
'You can get showered in your own time.' Ken grunted and left the room without closing the door.
'Hmm,' thought Belinda, 'he's going to have a peeky pie probably, don't know why, he's seen all I've got already and many times at that.'

Next door Ken opened a hidden cupboard and switched on his video recording gear. He'd spent thousands on it and diligently he checked all the feeds, six from the bathroom, ten from the lounge, eight from the bedroom... if he ever got her that far. He'd ensured all possible angles were covered and dreamt of re-enacting many porno versions of his favourite TV shows - Game of Thrones, Breaking Bad and Dinner Ladies.
Belinda was however no slouch and had already clocked the multi-coloured AV wires crudely stapled to the walls. How she loved a

performance and a performance was what she was going to give her Regional Sales Manager; Yorkshire.

'Any towels Ken?' Belinda shouted dramatically from the shower.

'Towels… towels, God Belinda, I'm sorry, I took the last ones home for washing and I've not replaced them yet. Didn't expect to be using the place this week you see.'

Belinda rolled her eyes and didn't for one minute believe him and shrugged her swinging tits at the creaking camera blinking above Ken's head, 'You'll have to rub me dry with your bare hands then Ken!'

'Whatever you say Boss, I'll get the wine.'

Belinda finished showering and shook as much water off herself as she could. She sauntered bald naked and bold as brass through to the lounge and smiled at Ken. He said nothing. Ken handed Belinda her wine and pointed for her to sit on the table. He pulled the chairs away. Belinda took a quaff of the cold wine and whilst not of the same quality as a Chilean Chardonnay, it would do the job.

She leaned back resting on one hand propped behind her, opened her legs wide and relaxed on the wooden table, watching the shower water dripping from her hair and Ken eagerly observing her partially opened labial lids.

'Let's get you dried off before you catch your death of cold.' said Ken in a husky voice taking her wine from her.

Belinda thought, 'He's excited, I think I'm going to get my first penetration of the day after all, what a relief.'

Ken started to rub his hands over Belinda's breasts, stomach and thighs doing his unsuccessful best to dry her off with a few spare pieces of toilet paper. He then turned her over on the table and repeated the technique on her back, ass and legs pushing her legs wide apart as he did. He changed tactics when he reached her feet and started to suck her big toes. Belinda murmured some words in excitement, her big toes were one of her best ergogenic zones and she was quickly under Ken's crafty but artful control.

Ken started to strip off his business suit, shirt, tie and trousers still sucking Belinda's big toes; soon he too was naked. Belinda turned round on the table and studied him, he was massive in the cock area, she'd have to remember to call him Big Ken from now on.

Ken's tongue moved its way inexorably up Belinda's body until he reached her clitoris. There he paused for a few minutes giving her a proper doing and then moved onto her tits and nipples.

Belinda screamed in anticipation, 'Fuck me Ken, just fuck me, I need it so, soooooooooo badly, I've been a good girl all day, that twat of a TGWU Union man wouldn't release me! My orgasm is still building and building... please Ken just fuck me, do it now!'

Ken did his powerful best. His penis penetrated her in one fluid movement releasing Belinda's snowballing orgasm. Belinda locked her legs around the table's legs and held on for grim death. Ken pounded her hard, Belinda screamed,

'Harder, harder, don't stop now, keep going, I need a bigger orgasm, harder, harder.' They orgasmed together; Ken fell on top of her and sucked her nipples till they were totally over extended.

'Hope you're not back up to see the region for a month or so,' said Ken, 'I'll need some time to recover.'

Belinda smiled and thought, 'Big Ken, you're a good un!'

Chapter 11;

Cock-a-doodle-flew;

Belinda was running late, she'd slept in; her trip to Yorkshire had taken more out of her than she'd thought. Bella's new replacement called Maeve, smiled at her as she pushed the heavy glass entrance door open.
'Morning Belinda.' she said.
'Oh Hi Maeve.' Belinda replied stifling a yawn.
In her office she relaxed into her black leather swivel chair and reviewed the last few days in her mind. The pace was too intense, she basically hadn't stopped since her trip to Amsterdam and she knew she would burn out if she didn't start to manage her time better. Perhaps she needed a holiday, jaded wasn't a word she wanted to entertain, but perhaps a weekend break would be the answer.
A knock at her door brought Belinda back to the present. Bella popped her head around staring at her slightly askance.

'What are you looking at?' said Belinda... 'Am I showing a tit?'
Bella laughed and said... 'Belinda, you're the boss, it's all different now... you could sack me for disrespect, or non-performance!'
Belinda laughed, 'Do you really not understand the job protection laws of this country? Why I'd have to give you a couple of verbal (that would be nice) and written warnings, then you could take us to the Industrial Tribunal where you'd get a couple of million pounds pay out and we'd be forced to replace you with someone worse!! No, my team is my team, let's all get rich together, it's much more fun!'
'Speaking of fun,' grinned Bella, 'Hazel's 'Transport facility' is ready. It's all set for tomorrow lunchtime, departing the Pentra Heathrow at 3.23pm!'

Belinda laughed; she always enjoyed Hazel's company and her offer of taking the Glee Team on a free flight for Giselle's hen do had been very kind. Belinda's mind swiveled back to matters in hand. 'Bella, confirm Giselle only thinks we're having a few drinks at the Pentra tomorrow, our normal weekly review sales meeting.'
'Yes Belinda, I can confirm that!'
Bella and Belinda laughed.

Days later, Belinda poured the first bottle of ice cold Australian Chardonnay into three glasses which Paddy the barman had set down on their table. Hazel was due to arrive in thirty minutes and whisk them to her plane.
'Well, Giselle. I am so impressed with you that Tony and I have decided to promote you as the Key Account Manager for our new Russian interests thanks to Girgor Calanski's activities.'
Giselle screamed. She just couldn't believe it. What a wondrous thing to happen.
'Thank you so much, Belinda. Just think of it. All three of us have had such life-changing promotions in the past few weeks. Good things come in threes.'
They raised their chardonnay glasses as Hazel approached their table bang on time. 'Time for your trial flight girls, follow me!'
Giselle looked suspicious but Hazel's thirty year old Jeep was parked outside and the girls jumped manfully into it. It spluttered into action and Hazel accelerated down the tarmac. Five minutes later she pulled up beside a 1950's de Havilland transport plane, still sporting ex-military insignia.
Belinda Blinked;

Hazel had managed to squeeze the Glee Team into the remaining free space of the cargo hold. The transport plane was already full to the brim with weekend editions of 'The Guardian Magazine' due for distribution throughout the Costa del Sol for Sunday morning. The girls manfully belted themselves onto the netting down the hull of the plane, put on their helmets with intercom and gripped the bottom of the bench seats in preparation for takeoff.

Bella broke silence first,
'What the fuck is going on... I mean, this is not a luxury Lear jet, I mean, I feel like I'm out of a scene from 'Where Eagles Dare'... and lastly, where are the complimentary drinks and peanuts?'
'Oh don't be such a piss head Bella,' Giselle replied, it's only for ten minutes... it's a trial flight.... get it?'
Bella screamed suddenly realizing the irony of the situation, 'Giselle, we're flying to Southern Spain, it's your hen do! Next stop's the Torremolinos strip!'
'After that, anything can happen!' Belinda screamed over the intercom.
'The glee team on tour?' crackled Bella 'what can go wrong will go wrong!
Giselle Blinked;

The wheels touched, bounced and the heavy old plane glided to safety under the careful guidance of one of the most proficient female pilots Britain had ever produced.
The intercom spluttered into life, 'Welcome, static, static, static, to, static, Malaga, Hazel's Transport Airline, static, thank you for flying with us today, we know you, static, have a choice and welcome you back with open arms in the future... static static.'
The Glee team cheered, clapped and stiffly lined up to descend the metal ladder which had been placed on the outside of the plane.

Fifty minutes later saw them start Giselle's hen do celebrations in the outside bar of the Imperial Hotel and Sun Resort on the infamous Torremolinos strip. It was a glorious break in the Spanish sun and everything was going to get hot, hot, hot!
Their first waiter Miguel proved to be an excellent sounding board. Tall, thin with an elegant black moustache he was the perfect first target.
'Go on Giselle,' Bella whispered, 'dare you to fuck him first!'
Giselle rose to the occasion and Bella's dare by asking him to fondle her tits. He did immediately and quickly removed her bikini top, massaging her supine nipples.

Chapter 12;

Butch the Sunburnt Kid;

The girls got pissed extremely quickly on cheap, cold, green, Spanish wine from Galicia. The relentless hot poolside sun beat down on them as Miguel their waiter got them in a mood to party by subtly exposing their tits. Unfortunately he turned out to be their first damp squib of the early evening. The waiter just wasn't allowed to go lower than their navels... hotel policy and all that... he expanded by saying they hadn't received the training required. He tried to explain to them that the company had slated training courses for later in the year, but alas due to budget cuts, even they were not assured.

Disappointed the four girls downed their wine and moved out onto the strip. They were so pissed they didn't care that large portions of their tits were now on show;
'We're the Glee Team, come and get us!' was their drunken mantra.
'I think, hic, the bloody Spanish Tourist board,' gurgled Hazel,' should pay for their fucking training... so to speak...'
'Yes,' chirped in Giselle, 'You Hazel as an official airline should lodge a bloody complaint... tell them they'll have no Sunday newspapers if they continue to piss you off!'
The Glee Team laughed in unison and soon spotted some red umbrellas overlooking the marina offering brief respite from the sun and dived under them.

'Quatro Gin and Tonics por favour!' shouted Belinda to the bemused waiter who came to serve them, slowly cocking an eyelid at their state of undress for so early in the evening.
'And four cocko's por favour.' shouted Bella not to be outdone. She knew she needed to improve her Spanish as Jim did a lot of business in Mexico.
'Four cockos,' imitated Giselle, 'Bella, what are you trying to say or are you just pissed?'

Bella stuck her tongue out at her fellow Key Account Sales Manager and thoughtfully drank up her drink.

Watching the girls from a strategic position on a nearby large black motor yacht was a youngish, but suave, heavily sun kissed Swedish gent drinking a stein of Skol lager. He openly laughed at the antics of the aging women in front of him and started to make comments in English about their inability to hold alcohol.

It didn't take Belinda long to pick up his running commentary on their party and she said,

'Hey guys, we've got an admirer… look behind you, its Butch Cassidy, the sunburnt Kid!'

Giselle, Bella and Hazel turned as one and immediately spotted Belinda's witty target. Butch the beautiful sunburnt kid went even redder than his wicked suntan would allow him. Giselle virtually swooned under the hot sunshine and slid gently off her chair onto the pavement. Within a flash Butch had jumped ashore, caught Giselle in his arms and gently sat down with her now ensconced on his lap.

Bella winked at Belinda and Hazel and moved her chair closer to Butch and Giselle. Butch in an act of friendship put his hand around Bella's neck and started to massage her shoulders.

Bella immediately ripped her bikini top away from her tits.

Butch dropped his hands and turned redder still.

'What's wrong playboy?' screeched the pissed as a duck Bella as she grabbed his yacht shorts bullseye. Butch fell backwards looking embarrassed. Belinda surveyed him over the salt rim of her margarita.

'I see you, little boy.' she slurred.

Butch looked into her understanding.

'You do?'

'Of course; even I was a virgin once.'

Bella's mouth had fallen onto the patterned plastic tablecloth; what was going on?

'Oh madam, thank you. You see, I'm here in Spain to get myself a couple of women who can teach me the ropes of standard sex... so to speak.'
Hazel laughed and said, 'Standard sex, standard sex with us lot, Butch you are joking.'

Giselle stumbled to her feet saying breathlessly 'Take me inside your yacht young man and I'll give your cock the engagement of it's life.'

Butch Blinked;

Butch handed out the cocktails as the four girls relaxed in the open cabin taking in the sparkling sea view. By now they had all undressed and were waiting to induct their host into whichever sex game he desired. Butch sat down between Bella and Hazel continuing where he had left off but with more abandon. True to her word Giselle took up her position and slowly pulled down his white yachting shorts with a nice piece of gold trim around the legs. She tossed them aside and got stuck into Butch's now randy penis.

Belinda observed all the action and wondered where she could pull her weight, so to speak. Moments later she was spread-eagled under her student's feet, using his toes to stimulate her clit. Belinda started to climax, but she was cut short by Butch standing up.

'I'm sorry. I just can't in public.'

'What do you mean? This is a fivesome's dream' purred Giselle.
'Only one of us can claim his cherry.' said Belinda knowingly as she
pushed the Swede onto the cushioned sofa.

The glee team held a quick conference in the bridge. Bella had
found the captain's hat and was manhandling the spokes of the
steering wheel.

'Well I think Giselle should pick his flower' said Belinda. 'She's the
cluckly hen after all.'

'Agreed.'
'Agreed.'
'A-hic-greed.'

When they re-entered the cabin and informed Butch of his sex
mistress, they were shocked.

'No I want that one.' His pudgy finger pointed at Belinda.

She shrugged at Giselle. 'Hate to pull rank, but it's virgin's choice.'
as Butch the Sunburnt Kid guided Belinda up a staircase, fondling
her naked ass.

Giselle, though clearly put out, smiled at her new boss. She
understood and now you mention it, Tony would probably prefer if
she abstained from young flesh before the wedding.

At the top of the heavily varnished wooden staircase, he muttered 'I
like you very much as you are.'
Belinda turned round and kissed Butch on the cheek.
'Why Belinda,' he retorted, 'I can do much better than that.' as he
manoeuvred her onto a white leather bench seat. Within seconds
he had Belinda's legs wide apart and he placed his nervous cock
into her pinkie.

Belinda moaned in pleasure, taking the odd moment to direct the Kid's actions, much like a driving instructor on a busy A road.

Once his penis was safely inside Belinda's labia, he started to gently thrust and took the opportunity to make some small talk.
'What do you do for a job Belinda?'
Thrust;
'I'm an International Sales Director for a pots and pans company.'
Thrust;
'International?'
Thrust;
'That's interesting.'
Thrust;
'Can I have some work experience?'
Thrust;

Belinda Blinked;

Chapter 13;

A Schweinsteiger afternoon;

It was Friday morning when Des Martin knocked on Belinda's office door.

'Hi Boss, how are you feeling this morning?'

'Busy Des; busy.' Belinda replied brusquely, quietly nursing the mother of all hangovers, it'd now been a full week since the Costa del Sol fiasco and all that Swedish booze. 'Des; todays clients... what's the score?'

They're actually old fashioned rag and bone men...'

'Very good Des, shall I ask the question again, what's the score?'

Des took a few minutes to clear his mind of Belinda's tits, how could he explain it,

'Well let's put it this way, you've heard of Pricekeen and Bargain Store... well these guys supply them with some of their products and they've got us out of a few holes in the past.'

Belinda started to become more interested.

'Go on Des... and...'

'OK, let's suppose Stirling Corp. orders 45,000 units of one article in our Oxy Brillo range. Now the factory says, to get the best profit from the deal we need to make 50,000 units. OK, with me?'

Belinda nodded.

'Now, Stirling's don't want 50,000 only 45,000 so what do we do with the extra 5,000 units.'

Belinda finished Des' sentence, 'We sell them to these lot at a much discounted price and they push them out to the discounters.'

'Correct Boss!'

'Good answer Des, now, how's the wife?'

'Gone, gone, gone... divorce finalised next month, house under offer and we're both out.'

'Ahh, so you are now one of the country's marriages ending in divorce. Statistics don't lie as any good businessperson knows.'

'Yes; but you've been a big help Boss.'

'Don't you mean your physical attraction to my gorgeous body?'

'Yeahhh...' Des looked at Belinda's breasts with a sideways glance, 'if we crack this account can I see all of you naked, touch all of you naked, and fuck all of you naked?'

Belinda thought of Ken Dewsbury and replied,

'Only... if we get an order from these people today.'

Des made excellent time on the journey and as the car slowed, he took a sharp left hand turn and stopped outside two large metal gates. They started to slowly open and Des drove the Jaguar slowly through them. Remote video cameras followed them down the mud road and Belinda wondered what she was getting herself into. The car stopped outside a big green dilapidated warehouse. It looked like what it was, a remnant of the Second World War.

'Come on Boss; let's get inside before the dogs smell us.'

Des grabbed Belinda's hand and literally dragged her through a shabby doorway. Her eyes quickly grew accustomed to the murky interior; it was full of large wooden crates. Des pushed on into the warehouse. At the far end Belinda could hear the noise of fork lift trucks moving around. A door opened to the side halfway down and a biggish man walked out.

'Hi Hans, great to see you,' said Des, 'can I introduce you to my Boss, Belinda Blumenthal.'

Hans proffered a hand, 'Hello, I've heard so much about you... welcome to bargain basement land!'

Belinda smiled and shook his hand, it felt cool and dry, not slimy and sweaty as she'd expected from a rag and bone man.

Hans ushered them through into the small office where a spluttering gas fire did its best to keep the damp building at bay.

'Greta, come and meet Belinda... Steele's Pots and Pans...'

A tall slim dark haired lady came out of a second room, she was absolutely stunning. Belinda held back a hasty gasp of admiration; it didn't do to greet new clients with one's tongue hanging out.

'Oh Hi Greta,' said Belinda taking her proffered hand.

'Hi Belinda.' replied Greta looking Belinda up and down with an appraising air.
Belinda definitely wanted to give her all she had... in discount terms of course.

Hans and Greta were brother and sister; their parents had set the company up many years previously and after ensuring that their two children had the necessary education and experience, had quietly retired to the heat of the Bahamas.
After a very quick tour around the warehouse, there wasn't much to see apart from wooden crates, Belinda nodded her head sagely. Whilst this was a down market business to her, and one that wouldn't increase her bonus one whit, the company did need to have this safety valve. Besides Hans and Greta interested her, their immaculate facial bone structure, the fact they were brother and sister and last but not least that they were both unattached, meant all things were possible...

But Belinda was also becoming more and more impressed with Des Martin. No one at head office had even hinted at the existence of this underbelly, but Des had had the balls to take her into the lion's den and boy, she couldn't believe the opportunities she'd encountered. Greta was just unbelievably beautiful, whilst Hans was so male, so masculine, she could have made love to both of them there and then in their disgusting working conditions.

Just then Hans told Des he'd just been delivered some interesting prototype items from Bisch in Germany, Steele's biggest European competitor and did he want to have a look at them. Des nodded eagerly, he used to work for Bisch a long time ago and always enjoyed seeing what they were up to even though he thoroughly disliked their ethos.

'You don't mind Boss, do you, it'll only take me forty minutes to take some pictures and make out a competitor report.'

Belinda smiled inwardly and replied, 'No Des, go and do your job, I'll have a cup of tea or something with Greta here.'

'Tea? Belinda, I think I can do better than that, what about a drop of Chilean Chardonnay?'

'Perfect Greta... after all Des is driving!'

The lads left and Greta went into the back room.

'Hey Belinda, what do you think of this... come and have a look.'

Belinda went through, Greta was holding out an exquisitely sexy brassiere in black lace.

'Got a crate of them this morning from Tokyo... try it on, I think it's your size.'

Belinda Blinked;

'I generally find Japanese stuff a tad small for my somewhat larger breasts.' replied Belinda rapidly taking off her jacket and blouse.

'No, trust me... I'm an expert, and this one will fit you beautifully... tell you what, if it does you can keep it... it's my size as well.'

Belinda salivated, removed her own bra and let her tits fall to freedom.

Greta gasped, 'Oh My God, what an astounding pair of breasts you have Belinda, may I feel their weight in my hands?'

'Of course Greta darling; would you mind reciprocating?

'Fuck me Belinda,' cried Greta reaching into the bottom drawer of a desk and pulling out a largish black dildo. Belinda removed her skirt, thong and heels... in that order, and quickly strapped on the hard wooden sex implement.

'Nice piece of kit, Greta....'

Greta panted back 'Also got them in this morning from New Guinea. Now stop talking and just fuck me Belinda!'

Belinda helped Greta onto a dark wooden crate sitting in the corner of the room, pushed her thighs apart and rotated the large dildo into her already sopping vagina. She clamped her mouth onto Greta's right teat and started to vigorously move in and out. Greta quietly screamed in ecstasy.

After about three minutes of frenzied activity and a couple of extremely wet orgasms Greta waved her free hand in submission saying,

'Stop… it's your turn now for ravishment Belinda.'

The girls swopped over, and it was Belinda's turn for violent release. No man had ever been this good, but then she'd never experienced anyone from New Guinea.

Chapter 14;

Belinda's Spiral Staircase;

Belinda and Des had arrived back at Belinda's central London
apartment. Des killed the engine and Belinda opened the car door
and swung her legs out.
She turned and strode the few steps to the concrete spiral staircase
which linked the garage to the first floor of her apartment. She sat
down seductively on the third step, kicked off her black leather
heels and ensconced her long supine toes around the metal railings.
Satisfied she had a good grip she lay back and stretched her arms
upwards. She again felt for the metal stanchions of the spiral
staircase and wrapped her hands tightly around them. Now, lying
prostrate on the steps, she weakly called out,
'I'm here Des! Come and take me!'
Des looked up from his fascinating digital dashboard and gulped. He
shook his head in disbelief, after all he'd failed to get a direct order
from Hans and Greta. He quickly stripped off; at last he thought, at
bloody last. He took his very healthy penis in his hand and started
masturbating it as he advanced upon Belinda. His foreskin went up
and down revealing more of his shiny knob with each movement.
'What stunning legs you've got Belinda.'
'Des if we're to do this right, I need you to call me 'Boss'... OK?'
Des gulped again, many tangled thoughts crossed his mind, but the
goal of screwing, 'The Boss', as he would now have to continue to
call her, was uppermost.
'Yes Boss... can you help me with the bra?'
Belinda groaned and lent forward, Des pulled her jacket off as best
he could, followed by the blouse, he didn't mean to rip it, it just sort
of happened in his haste to get to her gorgeous tits.
'Sorry Boss, I'll get you another... a stronger one...'
'Don't fucking bother,' replied Belinda now becoming slightly
amused, 'I only expect a week's wear from these rags anyway.'

Des grinned and continued his advance on Belinda's pulsating breasts.

But Des wasn't fully reading Belinda's mind speed, he was enjoying her nipples too much to think of her clit at the same time. However he did have enough basic sexual instinct to start proceedings on that region of her body with his fingers. He was soon roughly in the right place and started to rub the fleshy and quickly moistening mound. Des felt Belinda starting to breathe more deeply, he was doing good he thought, as he moved his lips and mouth to her left nipple. There he contentedly sucked and soon started to twirl his tongue around the hardening flesh. Lost in his lust, he inadvertently clamped his teeth on Belinda's nipple for a millisecond.

'God, Des!' Belinda shrieked, 'I'm not a bloody dummy teat!'

'Sorry, sorry Boss,' Des mumbled with his mouth still full of tit.

'Never mind,' whispered Belinda, 'it's not the first time... hopefully not the last.'

Des smirked, knowing full well he was lucky to get away with his sexual clumsiness.

Des' tongue replaced his inexperienced sticky fingers in Belinda's labia. He couldn't resist a quick slurp of the vaginal liquids now running freely from her body. They tasted divine, so much sweeter than that of his Ex... not that he'd been able to dine at that particular table recently.

'Des, sorry to interrupt...'

Des pulled his dripping face out of her vagina, looked quizzically at Belinda and said,

'Sorry Boss, have I done something wrong?'

'No, no,' replied a blushing Belinda,

'How's that Boss?' he asked feeling fearful.

'Not bad for a divorcee.' retorted Belinda subtly shifting her ass to find a more comfortable position than she had to date on the concrete step.

Des continued to titillate Belinda's clitoris. He'd decided on a two part operation, firstly one of stimulation and secondly a basic clean up. So after a period of tonguing he would embark on a slurping session which effectively cleaned up the juices recently produced. In order to keep a semblance of professionalism he did his best to maintain the slurping noise to a minimum, in actual fact it turned out to be a case of broad sucking.

The problem was, Des was not a leader, only now was Belinda starting to understand this facet of his character. If she wanted penetration, then she'd have to instigate it and soon.
'Des... Des, I need you inside of me...' Belinda whispered in a hazy type of way.
Des understood immediately, phase two was about to begin he thought.

Des Martin, recent divorcee and Regional Sales Manager London and South East for Steele's Pots and Pans fell to his knees and with his erect cock slowly started to penetrate his Boss, Belinda Blumenthall's already very wet vagina. He unbelievably slid in with no bother at all and started to slowly fuck her. They both groaned as their lower bodies met for the first time.
Des wasn't getting much friction, but he couldn't very well complain like he used to do, to his Ex. Perhaps he thought in a sad way, that was why she left him.
But Belinda was now perspiring freely and the grip her hands and toes had on the metal stanchions of the concrete staircase were becoming more and more tenuous. Belinda started to very slowly slide off her concrete step and as Des retracted for another stroke she suddenly slipped and slid the whole way to the bottom bringing Des with her. It was the chafing he needed and he came in a tumultuous rush of bright white semen and sweat. Bowled over by Belinda's weight Des was pushed onto his ass on the cold concrete floor with Belinda still riding his cock.
'God Des; that was a brilliant bit of athleticism, how do you do it?'
Des whimpered, groaned and looked up at his Boss grinding him into the cold hard floor.
'I'm just a natural,' he moaned, 'a bloody fucking natural.'

Belinda threw back her head, shaking free her long black hair she laughed exultantly, whilst experiencing a magnificent orgasm and finally extracted herself out of Des.

'Come on Des Martin, Regional Sales Manager Extraordinaire, get up, I've got a nice gin and tonic waiting for you upstairs, I reckon you deserve it.'

Des followed the seductive Belinda up the twisting staircase. As she wiggled her naked ass at him Des felt the stirring of something deep in his groin.

He thought, 'Oh God, nooo, she's going to fuck me again... what can I do?

At the top, Belinda took his hand and led him to her bedroom, where she reclined her stunning body on her purple water bed.

Chapter 15;

East Berlin;

Two weeks later...

09:17am
The grey leaden sky hung over one of the central Platz in East
Berlin. Large snowflakes slowly fell to the ground as Herr Bish made
the final changes to his meeting later that morning with his
Communications Director. He grimaced as he felt the twang of pain
shoot across his upper left arm. It was an unpleasant reminder from
his operational years of the cold war at the hands of a Western
secret agent. He knew he'd been lucky that day forty years ago, but
he could never bring himself to forgive The West or what they
stood for.

Herr Bish smiled as he shuffled his papers together, years of
preparation were now coming together very nicely. He sat back in
his large black swivel chair and hit the intercom button.
'Petra send in our agent immediately.'
Bish swung his chair 180 degrees round to face the large full height
window and stared out at the snow which was now falling much
faster. He smiled; his plan for espionage and very soon concrete
results, was about to start and here was his Special One visiting
him. His very willing espionage agent had been the key to
identifying an annoyingly pernicious competitor's impressive new
secrets. He laughed to himself manically, he was going to enjoy this
and he couldn't wonder why he hadn't gotten into industrial
espionage sooner... It was so much easier than inventing products.

The Special One strode into the room. Dressed from head to foot in
a patent black leather trench coat, she looked deliciously poisonous
and just the right person for this delicate operation.
'Gud mornink my Special Von.' Bish exhaled through his yellowed
teeth.

'Herr Bish, how nice to see you again, and so soon at that.'
'Yez my dear, congratulations on your rezent promotion. You have been zo successful so quickly, you may rightly expect a bonus...'
The Special One started to remove her thigh length boots and calmly folded them into a kind of leather roll before gently placing them into a corner of the office. Herr Bish licked his lips in anticipation of what was to come. He did love a good foreign thigh. East German girls just didn't do it for him these days. He quickly thought back to the days when they did do it for him... that glorious wall with all its intrigue, the sleazy bars built into its bricks with their underground passages leading to the West with all its cigarettes and American contraband.
The Special One slowly unzipped her black leather jacket, she was completely naked underneath and as she shook her magnificent breasts with their extending nipples free she placed the trench coat into another corner.

'Thank God,' she thought, 'at least Herr Bish liked women, she'd have had no chance against the large, smooth chested men who prostituted themselves for the chance to pull off an espionage operation such as the one Herr Bish had proposed to her. She didn't particularly like what she was doing, but she needed the money, friends, especially business friends... whatever they were, just didn't cut the mustard when it came to family.
Yes, family.
The Special One slowly pulled down her black leather trousers at last showing Bish her naked torso. She so wanted a fuck and she knew Herr Bish was up for it mentally, but she'd been let down so many times before. However she never gave up and as she tentatively approached Bish she saw him shudder in expectation and she sadly knew it was over. He'd found release in just seeing her naked, she reassessed the situation. She had to give Bish something; he was paying her big money, and a quarter of it that afternoon, her advance so to speak on results yet to be attained. It would have to be a blow job. After all, she really didn't want to have to kiss his horrible cigar stained teeth never mind the fetid

breath. No, good ole clean cum was a much better option and she gladly took it.

The Special One slowly pulled down Herr Bish's soviet style trousers, she removed his black underpants and gently kissed his flacid cock. A small amount of semen still remained on his penis, she delicately licked it up in one fluid movement. Bish groaned in delight whilst grabbing her tits and relentlessly squeezed her nipples between his spindly forefinger and thumb. The Special One's mouth in response sucked up all of Bish's member, she gagged on fresh air and sucked harder trying desperately to produce some sort of friction between her tongue and Bish's cock. She rythmically moved back and forth whilst Bish screamed for mercy, the Special One smiled, this was so much easier than all of her other encounters.

Bish pulled her closer to him, he wanted to feel her gyrating ass, it was so responsive, so tender. He'd show her who was the boss, he knew he'd prematurely ejaculated, but he was the money and he'd make sure she always understood... If she lived that long of course...

Within minutes Bish had become sated with her body and pushed the now panting espionage agent away from his cold body. The still naked Special One stood in front of the now coughing old school German watching him feebly pull up the zip on his trousers. She wondered how much longer he had left in this world, she'd better get her money quickly and get back to the safety of her deep cover.

Bish pulled open a drawer in his desk and took out a tablet device. He powered it up and asked the Special One for her bank account number. He believed in paying his bills promptly, suppliers always appreciated it and they always gave you priority when you needed another job doing. It was the same with industrial spies and this girl was one of the best he'd encountered. Her day job meant she came into contact with some interesting companies and he could choose which ones to infiltrate as and when he needed... but this project was so satisfying in so many ways....

Herr Bish tapped in the numbers and hit the return key.

'That's zit, my Special One, one million Euros now in your chosen bank account. I presume you haf expenses to pay and people to oil...

'Of course Herr Bish, there are always people to oil.'

Bish smiled, closed the computer with a flourish and watched her finish dressing. She was indeed a beautiful if wild creature, he wished he was thirty years younger and sadly shook his head. He reached for another cigar, lit it and inhaled.

'Gud morning Special One.' He waved her out of the room with his free hand.

'Until next time Herr Bish.'

'That will be soon, very, very soon.'

Bish coughed and took another drag of the cigar watching the now leather clad sexy ass depart from the room. Steele's Pots and Pans the Bish Herstellung's biggest competitor in Europe, indeed the world, would never know what hit them.

Bish cackled his cold, phlegmy laugh. Steele's brand new, top secret, state of the art Trioxy Brillo range would soon be his and make him a fortune...

Herr Bish Blinked;

The End;

If you enjoyed Belinda Blinked 3; then Belinda Blinked 4; will immerse you deeper into Belinda's sexual world of big business and the rich aristocracy... I promise!
Rocky xxx.

Hey... still drooling for more then why not let me send you some exclusive Belinda material. I've got some stuff which I didn't have room for in the books and you're welcome to read it. I also sometimes send out a newsletter with info about the main characters, a new book or podcast. It'll keep you up to date on the Belinda franchise and whet your appetite for more!
It's easy, just email me at flintstonerocky@gmail.com and I'll get back to you.
So this is what you get;
Material that didn't make this series.
A copy of Belinda's pay check, only Sir James, Tony and the IRS has this highly classified info!... well perhaps Giselle...
An occasional newsletter.
Advance notice of what's happening in Belinda's world!

Myself, Belinda, Giselle, Bella and Tony would love you to leave us an honest review. It really helps us to maintain our visibility in the book rankings. Thank you!

Sir James Godwin couldn't care less.... Hrrmmph;

If you haven't yet read Belinda Blinked 1 or 2, they're here!

BB1   http://amzn.to/2njv0Mh

BB2   http://amzn.to/2mQdVvK

You can also find us at

www.BelindaBlinked.com

www.RockyFlintstone.com

Or why not purchase the book My Dad Wrote a Porno
http://amzn.to/2mQhWjR
where you'll get lots of extra info on the podcasts!

Or enjoy the podcasts… find them on ACast or ITunes goo.gl/XgScSj

Or even splash out on some merchandise…..
www.mydadwroteaporno

Back to Contents

Printed in Great
Britain
by Amazon

31108280R00041